KU-034-181

THIS GIRL THAT GIRL

Charlotte Lance

ALLEN&UNWIN
SYDNEY · MELBOURNE · AUCKLAND · LONDON

This is this girl.

To Chewy,
because I'm like This and you're, like, all That.

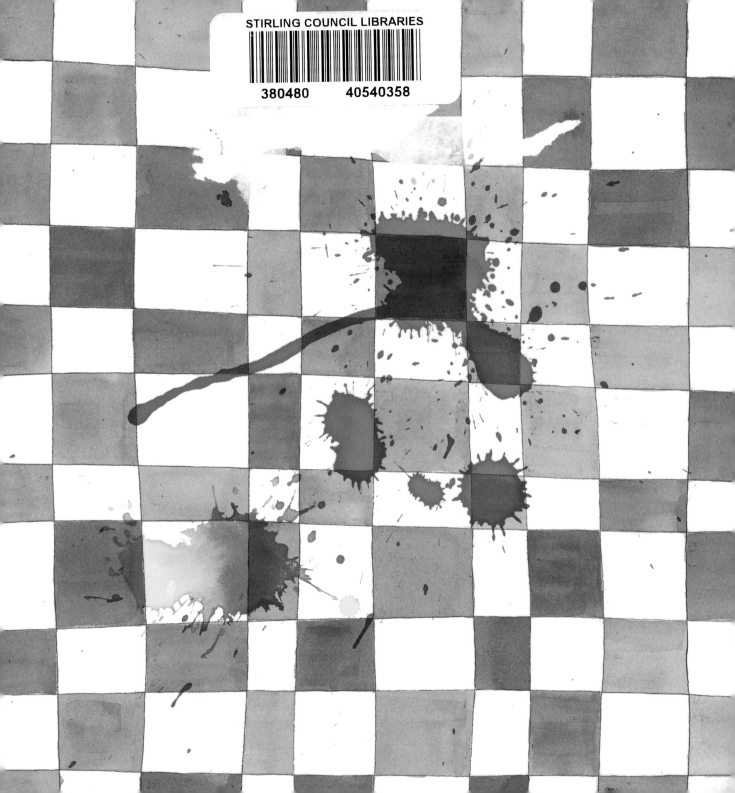
STIRLING COUNCIL LIBRARIES

380480   40540358

And that is that girl.

This girl likes to do things like this.

And that girl likes to do things like that.

This girl lives in that house.

And that girl lives in this house, next door.

That is this girl's dad.

And this is that girl's dad.

This girl's dad likes to do things like that.

And that girl's dad likes to do things like this.

So while this girl was adjusting
the grass, like this,

her dad was trying to fit into
a pillowcase, like that.

And while that girl pegged things to her mum, like that,

her dad separated the gravel, like this.

Last Tuesday, that girl's dad decided
he would build a treehouse like this.

This girl's dad thought it was a great idea
and decided to build a treehouse like that.

That girl gathered these tools.

And this girl gathered those tools.

That girl's dad gathered this timber.

And this girl's dad gathered that timber.

That girl sawed like that,
and her dad painted like this.

This girl hammered like this,
and her dad painted like that.

That girl did that, and her dad did this.

This girl did this, and her dad did that.

Until at last, these two...

and those two…

built this